The Christmas Trunk

Janice never thought she could hate her oldest brother, her best friend, her Christmas partner. But he was leaving her. The Army? Who was going to decorate cookies into the night with her? Sing every Christmas song? A hundred times each. And what about their favorite part? What about the tree? How could Edward not be thinking her? How could Janice possibly celebrate Christmas if he wasn't there?

The Christmas Trunk

A thank you, especially, for one special soldier

Holly B Barker

Columbus, Ohio

This book is a work of fiction. The names, characters and events in this book are the products of the author's imagination or are used fictitiously. Any similarity to real persons living or dead is coincidental and not intended by the author.

The views and opinions expressed in this book are solely those of the author and do not reflect the views or opinions of Gatekeeper Press. Gatekeeper Press is not to be held responsible for and expressly disclaims responsibility of the content herein.

The Christmas Trunk: A thank you, especially, for one special soldier

Published by Gatekeeper Press
2167 Stringtown Rd, Suite 109
Columbus, OH 43123-2989
www.GatekeeperPress.com

Copyright © 2021 by Holly B Barker
All rights reserved. Neither this book, nor any parts within it may be sold or reproduced in any form or by any electronic or mechanical means, including information storage and retrieval systems, without permission in writing from the author. The only exception is by a reviewer, who may quote short excerpts in a review.

The cover design and editorial work for this book are entirely the product of the author. Gatekeeper Press did not participate in and is not responsible for any aspect of these elements.

ISBN (paperback): 9781662913716
eISBN: 9781662914003

To all Veterans and Soldiers

I dedicate this book

Thank you for your service. For your sacrifices.

We are:

Home of the Free, Because of the Brave

And to:

My nephew TJ Barker 1982-2021

Your big, bright smile may have been bigger than your big, loud truck pulling into the cemetery each year. You will be missed when placing flags. You will always be missed. And you will always be loved.

Thank you

To my two editors:

Philip Newey

Joanne Crigamire

For your time and expertise

Thank you

To my three reviewers:

Tricia Pritchard

Rich Milner

Charles Castelluccio

For your time and kind words

And Thank you to my family

To my husband, daughter and son for reading my pages and giving me your honest opinions.

And to my, Husband-National Guard Veteran

And my Son-Army (Iraq) Veteran

Thank you for your service and for opening my eyes and heart again.

To remember, every day!

And to my grandchildren, for being there every year to help place flags.

I Love you more.

"Mom, you really don't have to make me breakfast every morning."

"I know," she quietly answered.

"I'm ok, really," Janice said, watching her leftover syrup slowly leaving her plate.

Mom's spatula turned as the egg-and-milk-soaked piece of bread sizzled louder.

Janice turned off the water. "Look," she said, raising her sweatshirt and showing her belt. "I had to move it from the hole I made to one that's actually in it."

The spatula clinked on the counter as a gentle smile formed on her mom's face.

"Thanks," Janice said. She rubbed her mom's shoulder. "Thanks for everything. But you know, I can pour a bowl of cereal tomorrow."

Her mom pulled a Kleenex out of her bathrobe pocket as she watched Janice walk away.

That "basement smell," used to hit Janice as soon as she opened the basement door, but for the past six months, it has been pine, and her dad's coffee.

At the bottom of the steps, she glanced to her right to see her dad back in his usual spot. The noise from his compound miter saw was a little too much in the morning so she hurried through an open doorway into a somewhat quieter room.

Sliding onto her stool, she could see her dad had already replenished her empty box. She reached in and picked up a palm size, dried, half inch thick, piece of pine trunk.

Staring at the flat, round piece, she glided her thumb over it. She felt its smoothness, its roughness, and the bumpy bark around its outside. Closing her eyes, she imagined when it was a tiny seed, its life so smooth and pure. As it began to grow, its lines, the circles, which she heard told its age, became a little rougher in spots. There were even knots, darker, more pronounced spots. She loved them but wondered if they reflected a time in its life when something bad happened: getting bumped or hit by a falling branch, or maybe by a kid. Perhaps an animal clawed it, or it went without water for too long. Could it have been the result of a terrible storm?

Or maybe it wasn't something bad at all. Maybe it was when one of the best things in its life ever happened. A kiss from another tree, a hug from a kid or a grown-up, a nesting spot for an animal, seeing a falling star for the first time, or having a hundred lightning bugs fill its branches. Maybe it was just having the best days of its life ever. *Christmas days*, she thought, wiping her eyes. *Christmas days for sure.* Janice smiled as she remembered one of her best times, of her favorite time of the year.

* * *

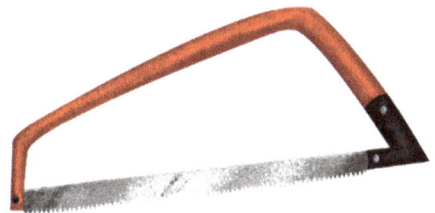

"Dad hurt tree?"

"No Twerp," Edward assured Janice when she was only three. "These are Christmas trees. This is what they were grown for and they know it and they love it." Janice shifted on her big brother's hip as snow fell off her little boots and her small arms wrapped tighter around his neck.

"They really love going home with people so they can be decorated and have presents put under them in their warm homes," he continued. "Just like this one wants to go home with us."

* * *

Janice's smile grew. *Yes, my ten-year-old brother did become my hero that day,* she thought.

"Is everything ok over here sweetie?" Her dad's hand touched her shoulder.

Drawing a breath as if she had just surfaced from the depths of the ocean. "I'm good," she said, shifting on her stool.

"Good," he said. "So, would you like a few more in the box or up here on the table?"

"On the table would be good."

His balanced stack of pine cookies became a fast game of catch-the-pieces.

"I got 'em," she giggled.

"I just finished cutting the very last trunk," he said. "I got forty-eight, nice, smooth, dried cookies out of it. I'll put the holes in them and hang 'em."

"Thanks Dad," she said with a small smile.

"You will have enough done," he assured her. "There's still five weeks before Christmas. You've done a lot. I'm very proud of you."

"Don't you two ever sleep?" mumbled a voice.

It was Janice's older sister, Rachael.

Janice laughed. "Where's my phone when I need it?"

"Bite me," said Rachael as she shuffled her big, fluffy, purple slippers over to Janice's table. Her long hair was up, well, some of it was in a hair tie. If there was one in there. She looked comfy in her pink and white striped flannel pajama bottoms and an oversized gray sweatshirt. Her thick, knee-length, plush, purple bathrobe completed her ensemble.

"Ok Barney," snickered Janice.

"Barney? Who in the heck is…Oh, ok, the kid show. So now I'm a big fat purple dinosaur?"

"Yeah, you kind of are." Janice smiled.

Dad did let out a chuckle as he put his arm around Rachael's shoulder. "Maybe the question should be, did you even sleep last night?"

"Ha, ha," said Rachael. "Aren't you two just so funny. And no, I didn't. I was working on that stupid paper for science class. It's driving me nuts. I thought being a high school senior was gonna be easier. And here." She emptied her hands. "I finished these last night."

Janice straightened ten pine-tree cookies Rachael had taken to her room and painted.

"You didn't have to do all these last night you know," said Janice. "You could have waited till after your paper was done."

"Ha, ha, ha, ha, ha." Rachael laughed crazily, smacking the table. "These kept me sane. I needed some sanity."

Janice and her dad looked at each other with raised eyebrows.

"Oookay," Janice said. "Well, you did a great job. I love the Christmas tree you painted. Dad, aren't these beautiful?"

"Very beautiful."

"Why don't you help paint, Dad?" Rachael asked, as she slumped even lower on the table.

"No." He giggled. "The art work I will leave to the artistic ones."

Rachael started half laughing. "Yes, yes. Remember that one time?"

"Ok, ok," he said, walking away. "Don't kids ever forget?"

"Not funny things," they both yelled.

"Well, actually, baby sister," Rachael said, "he really did try to help us the best he could with some of our school projects."

"He did," agreed Janice. "He really wasn't that bad. It's just fun giving him a hard time. And quit calling me baby. I'm sixteen you know. I drive. I do have my permit."

"Yeah, yeah, whatever." Rachael said ruffling up Janice's hair. "You will always be the baby no matter what age you are."

"Whatever," mumbled Janice. "Thanks again for helping me. For painting these."

"Sure, sure, you're welcome. I know Jack and I didn't love Christmas as much as you and Edward, but…"

Janice quickly jumped in. "Jack, yes, I hope he's doing ok. I bet he's not even up yet."

"Well, he never cared for school very much. You know that. He is trying," said Rachael. "College isn't easy."

"I know," added Janice. "But he can come home every weekend."

Rachael put her arm around Janice's shoulders. "Yes he can," she said. "And right now, I really need to get some sleep before I fall over. I love you baby sis." She kissed her forehead before walking away.

Janice sighed. When her mind refocused, she arranged the round pieces of pine trunk from the biggest to the smallest. *Christmas cookies*, she smiled.

* * *

Santas, snowmen, bells, stars, gingerbread men, reindeer and candy canes adorned the cookie sheet in the middle of the dining room table. It was loaded with naked, awesome smelling, and tasty sugar cookies. Bowls of colored frosting and containers of sprinkles were also scattered on the table. The beautiful decorated cookies lay close to each creator.

Janice and Edward's piles were always the biggest. She remembered Jack and Rachael lasting only maybe an hour, yet she and Edward always stayed as long as it took, decorating into the night and doing one of the things they both really loved, singing Christmas songs.

* * *

With "Frosty the Snowman" now stuck in her head, Janice picked up her pencil and carefully drew a line on one of the wooden cookies. She was hoping for perfection. She was hoping not to hide what is so beautiful on its own. As Frosty lead the kids down the streets of town, Edward lead her to one of their favorite places.

* * *

"This is so great," Janice said as she reached over and turned on the radio in her dad's truck.

"Yeah it is, Twerp," Edward said. "Crank up that Christmas music." His beautiful white smile and bright eyes sparkled, as he turned left at the end of their street.

"What the heck?" yelled Janice as cold air rushed in through Edward's open window. She covered all but her eyes with her scarf and hugged herself.

"Merry Christmas," Edward yelled out into the brisk air.

"Who was that?"

"I don't know?" He waved out the window as reciprocated, "Merry Christmases," were shouted back.

"You're crazy," giggled Janice.

"Your turn," he said. As Janice's window started going down she reached for her controls, but it was of no use. Edward's finger stayed on the button and her window was staying down.

"Edward!"

"Come on, Twerp, yell, tell them. Let everyone feel the spirit. I'm not moving till you do." And he was not kidding. People started honking their horns when the light turned green.

"Edward, really?"

All she got was raised eyebrows, so… "Merry Christmas."

"Louder," he said. "They're getting mad back there."

"MERRY CHRISTMAS," she yelled.

"Way to do it, Twerp," as he hit the gas.

The happy faces and shouts from the people made Janice happier too as they continued to shout, sing and laugh all the way to the best place around, William's Wonder Trees. It was sooo great that Edward finally had his license.

* * *

Janice set her pencil down and picked up her fine-tipped marker. She began retracing her pencil marks, again, wanting perfection. Just like that first tree. The first Christmas tree, just she and Edward picked out together, on their first trip alone.

* * *

"Where are you going, Edward?" Janice shrieked as he drove up the snow-covered roadway into the Christmas tree field. "The pre-cut trees are back down there." She turned back around in her seat with a confused look as the pre-cut trees along the fence disappeared from view.

Edward smiled a big smile, parked the truck, got out, took the saw out of the bed of the truck, and started walking.

"Wait," she yelled, catching up to him, "Dad said it was ok to cut a tree this year?"

"How about this one Twerp?"

"Oh, he didn't," she said, almost tripping over her own feet. "We haven't cut one down in a long time, Edward. Dad always made us pick out a pre-cut one. Oh, you're gonna be in big trouble."

"An old tradition brought back to new again," Edward said. "And no I'm not, miss chatter box. Right? This is our secret. So what do you think of this one?"

"I don't know," she said. "I'm not seeing it. And chatter box? Really? I can keep a secret. I can."

Edward walked around the tree, examining it from every side. "Come on, walk around it, check it out."

"Nah," she said. "I can tell from here, it's not the one. Besides, the snows a little deep around it. Not worth the walk."

"Come on, Twerp, step in my tracks."

He was not going to give up. "Fine," she huffed.

"Thank God you have feet like the Abominable Snowman."

"Abominable Snowman?" He laughed.

"Yes." She stopped right next to him. "And I don't think this is the tree. Look, there's a hole up there."

"Hmmm, maybe because there's too much snow on it."

Janice ducked, letting out a screech as the falling snow touched her neck.

"You're right." He laughed. "There's a small hole up there. A perfect spot, for a perfect ornament."

"Whatever," she said, shaking her collar. "I see a perfect tree over there." Giggling, the loose snow in her hands quickly took shape before it exploded on Edward's shoulder.

"Well, at least my Abominable Snowman feet will let someone know this is a perfect tree," he shouted. His snowball flying just inches over her head.

* * *

Janice held up the piece she was working on. *I was a good thrower and a good tree picker outer that day.* She smiled, approving of her craftsmanship. *Maybe not the best puller, but I was only nine years old. I was kind of little.*

* * *

"Timber," Edward yelled as the tree fell, spraying light snow in all directions. "Your turn," he said, sniffing something than sticking it in his pocket.

"What was that?" asked Janice.

"What was what?"

"What you smelled and then put in your pocket, you weirdo?"

"Oh," said Edward, pulling it out. "It's a piece of the tree." He held it up to his nose. "I love, love the smell of pine. And if you close your eyes and smell it all the pictures of Christmas come alive."

"You're weird," said Janice.

"And you're slacking. Come on! Mush girl, mush."

Janice grabbed the lowest branch and started to pull. She pulled, and pulled, until she was walking backwards with both hands on the tree. Edward turned the volume all the way up on his phone as their favorite Christmas tune came on and he sang out their version.

"Okay Twerp?"

"Okay," Janice sang out.

"Okay, Edward?" she added.

"Okay," he yelled.

"Okay Edward?... EDWARD!"

"Okay." He laughed.

"No. Okay help me," she panted.

"What, that's all you got?" He smiled walking towards her. "Ten feet?"

"Well there's so much snow and…"

"And what?" He laughed as he grabbed a branch. "Not enough muscle? Come on! You didn't think I was going to let you pull it all the way by yourself, did you?"

"I was hoping not," Janice said while trying to catch her breath.

"Twerp, we're a team," he said. They each grabbed the lowest branch opposite each other and pulled while continuing to sing their version. "Christmas is the best, best time. no matter what we get."

"So, another chipmunk?" Edward smiled.

"You're mean," said Janice.

"Come on, Twerp, aren't you ever going to forgive me? It was my brand new BB gun. I was only ten. And it was only one."

"You killed it," sniffled Janice. "One, plus probably more when I wasn't looking."

"Sorry I made you cry. For the hundredth time. I gave you a cute stuffed one for Christmas. And didn't you name it Edward?"

Janice sneered at him. "No, it's Angel. And for good reason." Pulling on the tree even harder.

Edward smiled as he quick stepped to keep up. She did forgive him, long ago. Especially after he did get her that cute stuffed chipmunk. But she didn't want him to know that. Smiling, they sang their last chorus. "Christmas is the best, best time, no matter what we get."

* * *

Janice stared down at the piece she was working on. Her "y" in "Merry" was a little squashed on purpose. It had to be. It was avoiding a spot where she knew a branch had been. Where she knew the tree was growing another part of itself. *Reaching for something, a way, to help support itself, or, more so, maybe to help others.* Something she wished, she had known then.

* * *

"No you won't," Janice could still hear herself yell. "Sandy, my friend's brother, went into the Army last year and he's only been home like twice. You can't come home on weekends and holidays like in college. Oh my gosh! You won't be home for Christmas anymore."

Janice hated Edward for the first time in her life. How could he just leave? How could he not be thinking of her?

* * *

She closed up the green paint and reached for the white. *The same*, she thought. I*t can't always be the same.* She dropped a few drops of white into the small green puddle on her paper plate of changed colors. Changed colors to fit her visions, to fit the way she thought would work best, and too fit the way she wanted. *Just like the changes she had to make to fit the black and white colors she was given back then.*

* * *

Eleven years old, and Janice felt like she was losing her best friend. Edward had just graduated from high school and he was leaving. He was supposed to stick around. He was supposed to stay close enough to watch Janice do all her things, and to cheer her on. Just as she had always done for him when he played sports. She knew she didn't make his decision easy. But it was not easy for her, at all.

She wrote many letters to him when he was gone, adding pictures she drew or photos of herself doing weird things. Rachael and Jack were ok. They just didn't get her like Edward did.

She would sit by the phone or the computer if she knew he was going to call. She played baseball, soccer, and basketball. The sports Edward loved too. Whatever it took, Janice kept busy. Yet dinner always came, nighttime always came, and so the emptiness never left. There was only one thing that could fill that emptiness, and thankfully, he did that as promised. Just days before that first Christmas, Edward came home.

"Come on, come on, Edward, hurry," Janice said as she headed up towards the Christmas trees.

"I think you'd better get going," giggled Mr. Williams. "The boss is calling."

"Yeah." Edward smiled. "With only a week before Christmas we have a lot of catching up to do, or should I say, *Christmasing* to do."

"Well, it's good to see you," said Mr. Williams. "And looks like a great thing for one young girl."

"My promise," said Edward. "Let's hope I can keep it."

And he did, the first two years.

* * *

Janice picked up another round piece of trunk as her pointer finger stuck to the edge, stuck on something sticky, stuck on sap. She reached for the canister of wipes on the table, wishing some things had been just as sticky, or stuck, back then.

* * *

"Your dad would really like you to go with us to get the tree," said Janice's mom.

"I'm not going," Janice said. "What's the sense?" she mumbled as her mom finally walked away from her bedroom door.

And what was the sense? Everyone lied to her, the recruiter, Mom, Dad. Even Edward. He wasn't coming home for Christmas this year. It was year three and he wasn't coming home. His unit was preparing to leave. Edward was being deployed.

Three and a half years he was in, but Janice labeled it as four. Well, the beginning of year four. It was the first week of February, and the first and last time Janice ever wanted this to happen. His family flew to his base as they watched his unit prepare to leave for war. Janice tried to be strong, for Edward. She even made sure they got a birthday cake to celebrate his twenty-first they missed in December, and her fourteenth in January. Janice didn't know how many more good-byes she could take, and this one was the worst.

* * *

The worst, she sniffled. *Not the worst, but it was rough.* Noticing some roughness on her piece of pine, she also noticed her flimsy, holey piece of sandpaper. Janice walked over to one of her dad's workbenches. She pulled open a wooden drawer and found a pack of new sheets. They were new, something that had not been touched, or felt before. *Like that day*, she thought. *I am so glad my dad asked me to go that day.*

* * *

"Janice," her dad said, "would you like to come with me tomorrow morning to the cemetery?"

"Cemetery?"

"Memorial Day is in a week," he said. "I'm going to be placing flags. I thought you may be interested."

* * *

Janice sat back down on her round wooden stool, pulling out a stiff, coarse sheet of sandpaper. Like that morning, those first feelings, and her slowly softening back then, the sheet too, slowly began to soften as she moved it over the roughness on the wooden piece in her hand.

* * *

It was 7 am. The cemetery was very still and very quiet as the gray sky above matched Janice's mood. She knew about Memorial Day, but she really didn't know.

It was a big cemetery. A very big, beautiful cemetery with vast open acres of beautiful, well-cut, bright green grass with headstones randomly standing, showing, and telling.

The barren spots, Janice knew, still contained a plot, a flat stone, another someone, or someones. But Janice's heart truly loved the wooded area. The deeper parts of the cemetery where narrow, dirt, stone-scattered roads ran through and up and around hundreds of headstones. Old and new ones shaded by beautiful, majestic maples, oaks, dogwoods, rhododendrons, and pine trees. A place she remembered her grandfather is buried.

With bundles of flags in their arms, the group of men that her dad had shared this day with for years, dispersed throughout the cemetery, and Janice and her dad carried their bundles while walking down one of the dirt roads.

* * *

Janice took in a deep breath as she held up her piece, testing its smoothness, and hopefully, unstickiness. As the pine smell filled her, she brought it to her chest, listening and hearing its story. Everything has one, and so does everybody.

* * *

The gravestones in the cemetery were so hard and cold, like the year the wars signified on their markers. Yet the names, the persons, the ranks, the branches, the ages, the very young and old were so real, so powerful, and so felt. Janice learned a lot that day about her dad, her grandfathers, other veterans and Edward. About their sacrifices for her, for everyone. She understood now why her dad had brought her. With her last flag, she gently slid it into a holder with less anger and more appreciation in her heart, as she whispered, "thank you."

* * *

Deciding to take a break from painting, Janice picked up her glue. Soon silver glitter was falling and sticking to the thin white layer like spreading fairy dust, or fake snow. She smiled, even giggled. *Christmas in July. Who knew?*

* * *

It was half way through his deployment and Edward was home on leave for two weeks. And Janice, well, she was definitely not letting the family get away without celebrating the Christmas he/they had missed together.

"Maybe the start of another new tradition, Twerp," Edward said as he and Janice turned into William's Wonder Trees on that hot July day.

"Maybe," agreed Janice. She could not take her eyes off her brother or the smile off her face. "Christmas was not the same without you. Let me tell you," she said. "I still jumped on Rachael's and Jack's beds at five o'clock in the morning. But it wasn't as much fun as when we do it together."

"Well, we can fix all that in a few days now, can't we?" He laughed.

The two sang Christmas songs for a whole week that July. (And Jack and Rachael thought they had dodged all that for one Christmas). They decorated their large back deck with twinkling Christmas lights, the four-foot waving Santa, garland draping all along the handrails and balusters, the seven-foot Christmas tree, and yes, fake snow. There were piles of scattered fiberfill, just about everywhere. Fake snowballs were either lying or flying around. And big flakes of white glitter sparkled on the red tablecloth. It was perfect. Presents were under the tree, and, yes, Janice and Edward happily did their early morning wake up ritual. Mom, Edward and Janice cooked all the traditional dishes, even the Christmas cookies. It was weird having it in July, but Janice realized it didn't matter when Christmas was, it mattered that everyone was there. And before Edward left, he and Janice made plans for Christmas *on* Christmas this time. She couldn't wait. His deployment would be over. So there were two things to celebrate. What perfect timing.

* * *

Janice let out a heavy sigh, blew her nose, and threw the Kleenex on top of the others in the garbage can. *How about some ribbon now,* she thought. She pulled over a box that held her pre-cut twelve-inch-long red and green ribbons. Choosing a red one, she folded the end and slid it into the hole at the top of the pine piece. Hole; a hollow place in a solid body or surface, a small or unpleasant place.

* * *

It was getting close to the end of Edward's deployment. It was six more weeks until Christmas, which meant only four more weeks until Edward was to be home. Until Janice heard, "Sorry." "Edward." and "Explosion."

Life stopped.

* * *

Janice pulled the three smallest pieces of pine trunk towards her. The almost last growth of the tree. *Was it done growing, though? Did it want to get bigger? Could it have gotten bigger and better if I or someone else hadn't cut it down?* she thought. *Or was it truly its end?* She pulled a green ribbon through.

* * *

Janice couldn't stop life from happening back then, because it just kept coming. School, birthdays, picnics, people laughing, everyone and everything just living. Nothing or no one would stop. Christmas could, though, at least at her house. She made everyone promise her, no decorating, no presents, no Christmas music, and especially… no tree.

* * *

With six pine pieces painted, sparkled and ribboned, Janice took them over to another part of the basement. Under one of the small windows was a table where pieces of cardboard lay, holding some of her finished projects. She moved them aside and replaced them with the ones she had. She then picked up a can. The smell was strong, but she was quick as clear polyurethane covered them-polyurethane that left a slight shine.

* * *

It was the second Christmas since…then. There was no music, no cookies, no Christmas food, no decorations and no tree. She was thankful her family was still honoring her wish, but…there was something. Something was shining that very dark morning, right where the tree used to stand.

Janice stood motionless. Her teeth clenched and her breathing quickened. Losing her appetite, again, she discarded her bowl of cereal on the counter and walked into the living room. She let out a sigh as her shoulders fell. On her knees, she ran her hands over the smooth, clear-varnished trunk. Then she smelled something. Her eyes began to well as she swallowed hard. Taking a deep breath, she lifted the lid. Another deep breath, she reached in, and gently detached the taped envelope. Sitting on her heels, the stove light from the kitchen was enough, as her trembling hands reveled its contents.

"Hey."

Janice jumped.

"Sorry, I didn't mean to scare you," whispered her dad.

Janice turned back as tears slid down her cheeks. "Did you do this?" she asked.

"Yes," he whispered.

Silence. Her dad was afraid to breath. *Did I screw up?* he thought.

But silence, if it continued, would have been better than what her dad heard next. Janice started to cry. Not a silent cry, but an emotional, cannot control sobbing cry. His heart sank as he found a spot on the floor next to her. They embraced.

"I'm sorry sweetie. I'm so sorry."

"No," she cried. "I love it, Dad, I love it. I just wish this pain would stop." Pictures, of family, and of her and Edward by their Christmas trees, slowly spread on the floor.

* * *

"How you doing over here?" asked her dad.

"Oh…Oh…Ok. Good," Janice half smiled as her hands slid under her eyes.

"Ok, just checking, sparkles." As he often did, whether she knew, or not.

"Sparkles?"

"Yes." He touched her forehead with one finger. "Sparkles. You look like one of your ornaments."

"Great," she said, wiping her face.

"Not helping," he said as his chuckle faded through the doorway.

Janice looked at her hands. *Silver and gold*, she thought. *Silver and gold decorations…on every Christmas tree.*

* * *

"Why do I have to go with you to the store?" Janice asked as she looked back at the TV. "This is Saturday. I don't go anywhere on Saturdays, Dad, you know that." *Especially right after Christmas*, she thought. *Come on, he knows that.*

"I'll buy you some ice cream."

"What about Mom, Rachael, the dog, a neighbor?" asked Janice.

"Your mom's baking and Rachael, well, you know, she's still in bed."

"You're not going to leave me alone, are you?"

"What do you think?" He always did try to get her to go out as much as he could.

Janice made a low growl and tossed the pillow off her lap. "Ok, fine," she huffed. "Fast! We're going to do this fast, and I don't need any ice cream. Maybe a candy bar, but no ice cream."

With a piece of chocolate melting in her mouth, Janice stared at nothing out the truck window. Then something caught her eye while they were sitting at a stop sign. *A chipmunk?* It was running around someone's front yard. It seemed to head straight for her when it disappeared into a…*Humph,* a *Christmas tree?* They drove a few more blocks before turning down their street as she counted six more discarded Christmas trees lying near the curb. *We did drive through here, didn't we?* Not remembering seeing any the first time.

That night, lying in her bed, Janice kept staring at her trunk. Then a thought, an out-of-nowhere thought, filled her as the emptiness still surrounded the lonely envelope in its bottom.

"Maybe" she whispered. "Yes, it would, it could. What do you think?" she whispered to herself, and Edward. Soon the worn, wrinkled, selfie picture of her and Edward and their first cut Christmas tree found the sheets, like her salty tears, as she drifted off to sleep.

"I think I had time for one cup of coffee," her dad said.

"Well, they might be picking them up this morning." Janice jumped out of the truck. "Don't the garbage men pick up the discarded Christmas trees?"

"Yes. And I know of people who take some to put in their ponds so fish have a place to hide." He came around the back of the truck. "Holy cow, hang on," he said, grabbing the tree and helping Janice to throw it into the bed of the truck.

"How many do you think will fit?" asked Janice.

"How many do you want?"

Janice had a plan, a Christmas tree/trunk plan. And when she found a silver-and-gold-glittered Christmas decoration in the bed of the truck, she knew…it was meant to be.

* * *

"Hey, baby sis."

Janice jumped, turning to see Rachael and Jack coming towards her. "Geez, nothing like scaring the crap out of someone," she said. "I thought you were really here, Jack." Rachael handed Janice her phone showing his smiling face.

"I am right here," he said.

"Ha, ha," said Janice.

"Well, I tried to call you on your phone first," he said.

"Yes," said Rachael. "I could still be sleeping."

"And you still could not be looking like Barney," Janice said.

"So how's it going, baby sis?" he asked.

Janice shook her head. "It's going, older brother."

"Can I see?"

"Of course." Getting off her stool, she walked him around, showing him all the finished ornaments.

"Wow, nice," he commented. "You got a lot done."

Before Rachael could open her mouth, Janice added, "With the help of Rachael and Mom, and, of course, Dad."

"That full box?" Jack asked. "Is that the one going overseas?"

"Yes," answered Janice. "I have to send it out Monday so the soldiers get it by Christmas. You are going to be here to help with the others, right?"

"Wouldn't miss it," said Jack.

"You ok?" asked Janice. "Do you like the school?"

Jack turned his head a bit while his fingers disappeared into his hair.

"Your hair's getting long," said Janice.

"Yes," he smiled tightly. "And school's going. It's going good." He smiled. "Ok, I'll let you get back to work. I'll see you in two weeks, ok?"

"Yes, ok," replied Janice.

"Love you, baby sis."

"Love you too, Jack," said Janice.

Janice stared at the wall after Rachael left, her mind elsewhere. Then the short, winter's day sun began setting, its rays shining through the small basement window, hitting the glittered ornament hanging on the basement wall. That fully glittered round ornament was the first found, and the one alongside all the other ornaments. The ones accidently left on the discarded Christmas trees they had picked up. Janice let out a big sigh. *Now,* she thought, *the finishing touch.* The most important part to her. The back, and sometimes front, of her ornaments. She hopes that these two words will let all the soldiers and veterans that receive one, truly know how much they are appreciated.

Picking up the wood-burning tool, she tested it on a piece of wood. "It's hot enough," she whispered, as she touched an ornament. A brown line permanently etched into it. *Permanent, forever,* she thought. *Permanent. Like tomorrow will always show.*

Setting the tool down, she reached into her pocket for a Kleenex, wanting tomorrow to come, yet not, and still asking. Why?

Sleep did not come easily that night for Janice. Her stomach was doing as many flips as she did on her mattress. Picking up her comforter, which had somehow found the floor, she wrapped herself in it and walked over to her trunk. The early morning was still dark, but her nightlight revealed her full trunk as she lifted the lid.

She was proud of herself. She loved what she was doing, what she did. The many trees they had collected from last year's Christmas were being used for something good. *Something really good*, she thought. She just wished it didn't have to be because…her face dropped into the comforter, along with muffled sobs, and her hand tightened, on an ornament.

When the sky started to lighten, and after her two bites of toast for breakfast, Janice and her dad headed down the road.

Soon, she was stepping out of the truck, her neck sinking between her shoulders and her arms tightening into her chest. With slow steps, she walked down the lightly snow-covered dirt road. Most of the trees held thin lines of white on their barren branches as the evergreens showed off their strength and beauty with as much snow as was offered to them. The quiet was beautiful and peaceful as Janice's deep breath exhaled an angel-like presence. The winter birds chattered to each other in the trees. "Oh!" She jumped. Even a chipmunk was out, running around.

Her steps were slow while her mind and her heart felt like they were in a race. The trees grew thicker and her arms pulled in tighter, preventing her from being swallowed up into another dimension. She was scared, and not of the cemetery.

Part of her felt guilty for not coming more often, but if she didn't see it, it wasn't true. Edward was still just away, away in the military. This…This was all just a bad dream.

Stopping, she closed her eyes for a few seconds, took in a deep breath, exhaled and turned. Her body shook, and not from the cold. Her blurred eyes read the name on the smooth, shiny, gray stone forty feet up the hillside to her right. The name. The name of the best friend Janice could have ever had.

Minutes, or a lifetime, passed before she unfolded her arms and her fisted, mitten-covered hands slid across each cheek. Slowly, not matching her heart, or tears, her steps drew her closer.

She straightened his flag and wiped the snow from the top of his stone, then stood.

"What…what…do you think…Edward? You like it?" The ornament dangled from her fingers. "I made this one special for you. I…I, made it out of a Christmas tree trunk." She half giggled and smiled. "And you gave me the idea. Yeah, yeah you did." She swallowed hard as her mitten absorbed more than just tears. "Putting that piece in your pocket that day, remember? Remember you weir…do?" She gasped, and her eyes closed.

"Hey, guess what? I know why Dad quit cutting our Christmas trees down, Edward. Yes, I know now, Edward, I know. He said it might waste the ones that had already been cut because they may never get used. But look…Look, now I found a use for them. I'm making ornaments out of them. Ornaments for soldiers and veterans. Dad loves them, and I hope you do too. I…I really…hope you do." She stared at, though, or beyond the shaking ornament.

"Did you see the trunk Dad made me, Edward? It's so beautiful. Dad saved our Christmas trees. It's made out of our Christmas tree trunks. Our trunks…Yeah, Edward…our trunks."

The ornament disappeared into her right hand while the box under her left arm crumpled against her side. "I wish you were here to help me make these, Edward. You would be so good at it. I mean, you taught me everything about Dad's tools. Well, Dad did too, but you helped me a lot. Thank you for teaching me so much. And Edward, I've been wanting to tell you I'm sorry. Sorry I gave you a hard time when you told me you were going into the Army. I was stupid," she cried. "I know now, I do. I know you were always thinking of me. You were thinking of everyone. I'm not mad at you anymore."

Her breath was becoming hard to catch. "I miss you...so...so much, Ed...ward. So, so much," she stammered as, "that" dark hole started opening up again.

Motionless, her dad reached in his left pocket for a dry Kleenex. *Should I give her more time, or save her?* he thought. *Save.*

"Are you ready for this?" he asked softly.

Janice's fisted right hand ran across her cheeks as she turned and looked down. "Yeah, Dad, I'm ready."

With the wooden box in place, Janice and her dad lined it with plastic, put some rocks in the bottom and then a layer of topsoil. They placed a small pine tree in the middle and finished filling it with another bag of soil. Janice then opened the small box, pulled out some Christmas lights and ornaments and decorated the tree. Last, as she placed the Christmas tree trunk wooden ornament near the top of the tree, a chipmunk darted out of nowhere. He ran back and forth, chattering like crazy.

"I think he's telling you he likes it," said her dad.

"Maybe," said Janice. "Or, he sees something new he wants to destroy. Besides, I thought they hibernated?"

"Yes, they normally do," he said. "Maybe he's a confused one."

"Merry Christmas" was in red and green paint on one side of his ornament along with a sparkly angel. Janice gently touched the burned words on the back. 'I will never forget you. Thank you. I love you, Twerp.' A name she missed. A name, she knew, she would never hear again.

After promising Edward she was coming back on Christmas day in four weeks, she and her dad walked away. She turned to look at his tree, and him, one more time. There, sitting right on top of Edward's stone was that chipmunk. He was looking right at her and still chattering away.

Oh, she thought, *please don't ruin anything, especially his ornament.*

Jack came home on his Christmas break. He was excited, and honored to help Janice fulfill a part of her goal while he was home. A week before Christmas, Mom, Dad, Rachael, Jack and Janice walked into their local veteran's hospital, carrying boxes of their tree/trunk ornaments.

About two hours later, they walked out of the building in silence. Mom and Dad walked ahead as Dad's arm pulled her in tight. Rachael's phone went off. Janice and Jack were in the rear.

"You ok?" Janice asked, looking up at his face.

"Yes, I'm good," he said, slightly turning his face away from her.

Janice stopped and grabbed his arm. "Jack."

"What? I'm good, really."

Janice let out a sigh. "Jack, I know you hate that school. I know you hate college. I see it. I feel it."

"It's ok," he mumbled. "It's ok. I'll get it. I'm getting it."

"NO," she said louder. Now she stood right in front of him. "I was selfish, I was wrong, Jack. You don't belong there. I know it and you know it. Your eyes lit up in there talking to all those veterans. It's you, Jack. It's in you, it's in your blood. Edward, Dad, Grandpa, Great Grandpa. Who knows how far it goes back."

He looked at her. He needed more.

She gave him a small smile. "But you know," she said, reaching up and pushing back the hair from his face. "This will all be shaved off."

The next morning Janice sat on her bed, paced her bedroom floor, looked out her window and then sat back on the bed. Letting out a heavy sigh, "Yes," she softly said. "Yes…Yes we should."

She walked into the kitchen as mom flipped a pancake. "Dad."

"Good morning," he said.

"Good morning sweetie," her mom added.

"Good morning," she said, picking at something or nothing on the edge of the island. "My trunk is empty. I…I…I think we need a tree."

Mom quickly grabbed the spatula before it found the floor. Her dad looked right into her eyes for a few seconds and said, "I think you're right."

Her mom walked over as their embrace felt like a long, lost best friend. Then Janice's eyes widened and her mouth dropped open. *Oh crap*, she thought, as a blurred vision became clearer. The totes, the ornaments, and all the decorations. The storage room floor and shelves in the basement covered-covered with thrown, broken, and ripped up Christmas decorations. Janice didn't remember much of those first days, those first weeks, even months after the terrible news. But right now, as her stomach tightened, she did remember sitting on the floor in that storage room, surrounded by her hurt and anger.

"I hope I didn't ruin all the ornaments and decorations," Janice whispered. "I'm sorry."

"No, no, no, they're fine. They're all fine. Everything's fine," her mom whispered. She knew they weren't, but what she eventually salvaged was enough.

Janice and her dad drove into William's Wonder Trees. She inhaled a deep breath. *Edward, I wish you were picking out this tree. You never got your turn,* she thought.

Slowly, very slowly, she got out of the truck and walked over to the cut ones lined up along the fence, while her dad and Mr. Williams talked. She walked back and forth, kind of looking at them, and kind of looking...

"Go ahead," said her dad.

"What?"

"Go ahead. Go up there and pick out a tree."

"We're going to cut one?"

"Yes, we're going to cut one. Besides, like you said, your trunk is empty."

"You know Edward is very proud of you," said Mr. Williams.

"Yeah?" said Janice. "I don't know? I don't know if he knows?"

"Oh he knows," said Mr. Williams. "He knows."

I wish he would let me know he knows, she thought, as the snow got a little deeper. *I really wish he would.*

* * *

"Edward, you put your sister down right now," yelled their mom. "You get down off that chair before you both break your necks."

"I had to put the angel on top of the tree, Mommy. Edward was helping." And he was. What four-year old can reach the top of the Christmas tree without being on her big brother's shoulders, and on a chair? "Are angels real, Edward?" she asked, looking way up at the silver-and-gold sparkling angel.

"Of course they are, Twerp." He put her on his hip. "They're always here and they're always looking after us. They may not all be leaning and as crooked as ours," as he swayed and tipped her, "but they're always here."

"Edward, Edward." She laughed, hanging on for dear life. "It's Mommy's fault. It's her fault. She scared me."

* * *

Scared, Janice thought. *Not scared right now, but it is kind of spooky.* No one was here. No one was anywhere in the tree field. With only four days until Christmas, why would there be? And why would there be any good trees left?

It was cloudy, and it wasn't snowing. There were about two inches of new snow from last night. Not bad. Janice walked down the wide center between the rows. She glanced up and down each row, walked a short distance into a couple, and then just stood. She was lost, and alone. Too alone. She didn't know what to do. Actually, now, she didn't know if she wanted to do anything.

Then she heard something. She looked to her left. "I know that sound," she whispered. She bent over and peered down the row. "Come on, I know I heard you."

"Ah, there, I saw you, I saw you," she said as she jumped. She did see the little guy. A chipmunk was chattering and running around in the trees.

She crept closer as he ran under and disappeared into a tree. She stood guard, waiting to be scared. But, as she was looking for the little guy, she noticed something else. Footprints. Footprints that went around the tree.

"Humm, someone thought this tree looked good," she said, "and not too long ago."

She examined the tree. "Not bad," she mumbled. "I wonder why they didn't take it?"

She checked it out, carefully stepping into the footprints. "I'm glad they had big feet." She smiled. "Abominable Snowma…."

She stopped, for two reasons. *This isn't possible*, she thought. Then her heart almost stopped.

"Is this the one?"

"Oh, hey, hi, Dad." She pressed her hand harder into her chest. "Yes I think. Yes, this is the one."

"Well, it's a very nice looking tree," he said as he walked over. "A little bit of a hole up there, but it's beautiful."

"Yes…there is," she mumbled. "A perfect spot…for a perfect ornament."

Janice stood back as her dad cut it down. When the tree fell, he grabbed hold and started pulling while Janice grabbed the lowest branch on the opposite side.

"You don't have to help," he said. "I got this."

"I want to. I, I just…I want to help."

As soon as they had pulled the tree out of the row and into the middle path, Janice was surprised to see another family heading up their way. It seemed to be a mom, dad and three kids. Two boys and a girl. The oldest boy seemed to be in a hurry as he took off ahead of his family.

Janice figured he was around her age, fifteen or sixteen. His mouth was moving, as if he was talking to himself or something. *But, whatever,* she thought. *Most boys are weird anyways.*

As he got closer, he and Janice made eye contact for a second and he nodded before he came to a dead stop.

"Hey," he said, pulling an earphone out of one of his ears, "aren't you the one with the Christmas trunk? I saw you in the paper."

"Yes," she answered.

"Well, I have to tell you what you're doing is cool, very cool. I think it's great. Actually, you're the reason we're getting a real tree this year, so thank you. We haven't had one in forever. And we're going to bring it back here so you can have it when we're done."

"Thank you," said Janice. "I'll definitely use it to make more ornaments."

"Yes, thank you," added her dad.

"Well, you can't do it all alone," said the boy. "Like you said in the paper. There's a lot more veterans and soldiers out there. Oh." The boy jumped. "Look." He pointed. "Look at that crazy thing."

About ten feet in front of them there he was, a chipmunk, *that* chipmunk. Janice was sure it was the same chipmunk. He was chattering and darting back and forth in front of them as if he didn't know which way to go.

"Wow," said Janice's dad, "another one?"

"Alvin," the boy said.

Janice shot him a look. "What?"

He pulled a phone out of his coat pocket and pulled the jack out of it as Janice heard her and Edwards once favorite tune.

"Alvin," he said, starting to walk away. He belted out the last chorus as Janice mouthed her and Edward's version they had made up when she was only four. "Christmas is the best, best time, no matter what we get."

However, this year, it truly did matter. Janice smiled.

AUTHOR BIO

Holly Barker, who's favorite holiday is Christmas, incorporates her feelings when placing flags for memorial day, with the giving spirit of Christmas, to recognize and give thanks to Veterans & Soldiers that have given to her, and everyone, in her book, "The Christmas Trunk." Holly lives in Titusville, Pennsylvania with her husband of 36 years. Every year their two children, four grandchildren and extended family place flags for memorial day. A tradition that has been carried on in the Barker family for 80 plus years.

www.ingramcontent.com/pod-product-compliance
Lightning Source LLC
LaVergne TN
LVHW072013060526
838200LV00059B/4668